For Matteo, the newest member of our family

DIAL BOOKS FOR YOUNG READERS
A division of Penguin Young Readers Group
Published by The Penguin Group
Penguin Group (USA) Inc., 375 Hudson Street, New York, NY 10014, U.S.A.
Penguin Group (Canada), 90 Eglinton Avenue East, Suite 700, Toronto, Ontario, Canada M4P 2Y3 (a division of Pearson Penguin Canada Inc.)
Penguin Books Ltd, 80 Strand, London WC2R 0RL, England
Penguin Ireland, 25 St. Stephen's Green, Dublin 2, Ireland (a division of Penguin Books Ltd)
Penguin Group (Australia), 250 Camberwell Road, Camberwell, Victoria 3124, Australia (a division of Pearson Australia Group Pty Ltd)
Penguin Books India Pvt Ltd, 11 Community Centre, Panchsheel Park, New Delhi - 110 017, India
Penguin Group (NZ), 67 Apollo Drive, Rosedale, North Shore 0632, New Zealand (a division of Pearson New Zealand Ltd)
Penguin Books (South Africa) (Pty) Ltd, 24 Sturdee Avenue, Rosebank, Johannesburg 2196, South Africa
Penguin Books Ltd, Registered Offices: 80 Strand, London WC2R 0RL, England

The publisher does not have any control over and does not assume any
responsibility for author or third-party websites or their content.
Designed by Teresa Dikun and Jasmin Rubero
Text set in Aunt Mildred
Printed in the U.S.A.

3 5 7 9 10 8 6 4 2

Library of Congress Cataloging-in-Publication Data
Soman, David.
Ladybug Girl and the Bug Squad / by David Soman and Jacky Davis.
p.   cm.
Summary: When Lulu invites her friends from the Bug Squad—all dressed
up as insects—to come over for a playdate, she wants everything to go
just as she has planned.
ISBN 978-0-8037-3419-7 (hardcover)
[1. Play—Fiction. 2. Cooperativeness—Fiction.] I. Davis, Jacky, date. II. Title.
PZ7.S696224Lc 2011
[E]—dc22
2010011880

Ladybug Girl
and the
Bug Squad

by David Soman and Jacky Davis

Dial Books for Young Readers
an imprint of Penguin Group (USA) Inc.

"I can't wait for everyone to get here!"
yells Lulu. It is the first official Bug Squad playdate,
and Ladybug Girl knows it's going to be perfect.

"I know exactly the way I want everything to be!" Lulu tells her mama.

"Well . . ." her mama says, "I hope it works out the way you want it to, Bug-a-boo."

Just then, Sam comes bounding through the door.
"Bumblebee Boy is here!" he shouts.
Next, Marley, dressed up as
Dragonfly Girl,
skips in with Kiki in her
Butterfly Girl costume.
Everyone twirls around,
and shows off their wings and capes.

"The Bug Squad is a team again!" Lulu says.
"What should we play?" asks Sam.

"Bug Squad, of course," says Lulu.
"Let's go to the Bug Squad base!"
They pass Lulu's brother on their way out.
"He doesn't like bugs," Lulu says.

NO BUGS ALLOWED!

Lulu leads the group to a circle of tall
pine trees in her yard.

"This is it!" says Lulu.
The low-hanging branches and the soft
carpet of pine needles make the perfect hideout.
"I like it," says Sam.
"It smells good," says Marley.

They set up their base; Bumblebee Boy
and Dragonfly Girl zoom off to collect sticks
to defend the Bug Squad from bad guys.

"Let's go pick flowers to make it pretty," says Butterfly Girl.
Ladybug Girl says, "Bingo, stay here and guard the fort."

When the base is ready, it looks even better than Lulu hoped.
"Now we need a password to get in our secret hideout,"
she tells the Bug Squad. "And I know just what it should be:
Ladybug Rainbow Unicorn!"
Sam wrinkles his nose.

"What about Bingo for a password?" suggests Marley.
"Yeah, Bingo!" everyone yells.
Lulu agrees that it is a good password.
"Now what should we do?" asks Kiki.

"It's time to show off our powers!" decides Lulu.

"I'll go first!" says Marley.

"Dragonfly Girl breathes fire,
    so I can protect us!"

Swirling her flame around, Marley adds,

"*And* I can toast marshmallows!"

Sam steps forward.
"Bumblebee Boy
is as fast as lightning,
and will sting anyone who tries to get us!"

"Did you know that Butterfly Girl
has smart powers?" quizzes Kiki.
"Butterfly Girl knows that
the sun is really a star.
And I can spell elephant:
e-l-e-p-h-a-n-t!"

"My turn!" says Lulu. "Ladybug Girl
has lots of powers. I can fly, I'm super-strong,
I can save ants, and I can even do a cartwheel!"
Her try is a bit wobbly.

Lulu leaps to her feet and says,
"Follow me! Let's play
'We Can't Touch the Ground Because It's Hot Lava.'"

They safely cross over the lava,
but now an army of giants bars their way.

Luckily they're asleep, and the Bug Squad
carefully tiptoes past them.

"We made it!" yells Lulu. This is the best playdate ever, she thinks as she runs and jumps with Bingo and her friends. Everything is going just how she wanted it to! They are flying and laughing when Lulu's mama calls, "It's painting time!"

At the picnic table they find a pile of smooth rocks, a stack of paper,
and jars filled with bright paint.

"Now it's time to make Bug Squad pictures!" announces Lulu.
Lulu, of course, paints her rock red with black polka dots.
She is very pleased with how it turns out.
Maybe it should even be in a museum.

Kiki paints her rock purple. "This is Pluto!"
Marley is painting a pretty dragon playing soccer.
Sam is painting a picture of a robot
fighting a giant squid.

No one paints Bug Squad pictures, except for Lulu.
"Hey, you guys were supposed to—" Lulu starts,
but then Mama comes over with a platter.

It is filled with beautiful chocolate cupcakes.
Mama sets the cupcakes on the table and lights the candles.
"Now," says Lulu, "when I count to three
we all have to blow out our candles
at the very same time!"

Lulu counts "One, two, three!"
and blows out her candle.

Then she sees Kiki's candle
still flickering.
Lulu leans over and blows out
Kiki's candle too.

Lulu takes a big bite of her cupcake
and notices that Kiki hasn't even
picked hers up.
"What's wrong, Kiki?" Lulu asks.

"You blew out my candle!" Kiki shouts.

"But I was just trying to help you," explains Lulu.

"You didn't blow out your candle at the **right time!**"

"I didn't have to do it **your** way. I was making a wish, and **you ruined everything!**" yells Kiki.

Lulu's stomach feels funny.
She didn't mean to hurt Kiki's feelings. She'd never want to do that in a million years. It's just that she was having so much fun that she didn't think twice when she blew out Kiki's candle. Lulu just wanted things to be the way she had imagined them.

Now that she sees Kiki is upset, Lulu wants her friend to know how sorry she feels. But what if Kiki doesn't understand?

Then Lulu remembers that Ladybug Girl
never runs away when things get hard.
Ladybug Girl knows what she must do!

Ladybug Girl takes a deep breath and says,
"Kiki, I'm sorry I blew out your candle."

Ladybug Girl adds,
"How about if we ask Mama to light yours again?"
"Well . . . okay," agrees Kiki.

When the candle is lit, Ladybug Girl says,

"You can blow out your candle now, Kiki, and make a wish!

I mean, if you want to!"

"I do," says Butterfly Girl.

"Let's blow the candle out together!"

When they finish their cupcakes, they decide it's time
for a very important, secret **Bug Squad** mission.

"There's a mean alien in the house," says Ladybug Girl, "and we have to find out what he's up to..."